# MRS. WIGGLESWORTH'S SECRET

Written by Robyn Supraner

Illustrated by Paul Harvey

## Troll Associates

Troll Associates, Mahwah, N.J.

Library of Congress Catalog Card Number: 78-18041

# MRS. WIGGLESWORTH'S SECRET

I have always wanted to be a private
eye. I love mystery. I love adventure. I love
excitement. Also, I am a very nosy person.

You cannot keep a secret from me.
Don't even try. If you do, I will snoop
around. I will ask a lot of questions. I will
poke and pry until I find out what I want to
know.

Take Mrs. Wigglesworth. She thought
she could fool me. She was wrong. Mrs.
Wigglesworth lived next door. She's gone
now. She doesn't live there anymore.

It all began six months ago. The
Browns, who used to live next door, moved
out. Mrs. Wigglesworth moved in.

She was rich. I mean *super* rich. She had
a diamond crown and diamond bracelets
and a million diamond rings. When the sun
shined down on her, she sparkled like a
Christmas tree.

She wore her diamonds everywhere. She even wore them when she was driving her truck.

Oh. I forgot to tell you. Mrs. Wigglesworth didn't drive a car. She drove an old pickup truck. Strange, isn't it? But, as they say, truth is stranger than fiction.

Another strange thing. Her hair. It was red. I don't mean red like hair is supposed to be red. I mean red like red shoe polish. I notice things like that. I noticed other things, too. But I'll get to them later.

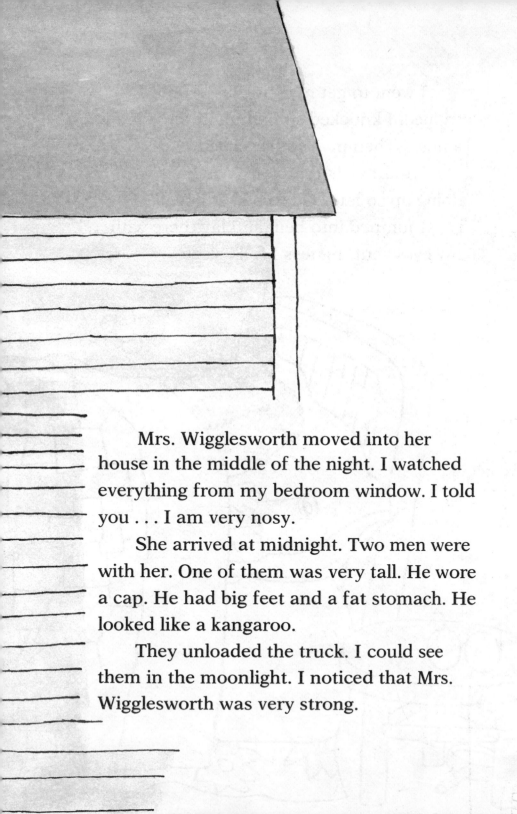

Mrs. Wigglesworth moved into her house in the middle of the night. I watched everything from my bedroom window. I told you . . . I am very nosy.

She arrived at midnight. Two men were with her. One of them was very tall. He wore a cap. He had big feet and a fat stomach. He looked like a kangaroo.

They unloaded the truck. I could see them in the moonlight. I noticed that Mrs. Wigglesworth was very strong.

I went to get my spy glasses, but I
tripped. I knocked something over. It made
a noise. Then my mother called,
    "Audrey? Is that you? What are you
doing up so late? Go to bed at once!"
    I jumped into bed, and lay there with
my eyes shut. I guess I fell asleep.

In the morning, I looked out of my window. I saw Mrs. Wigglesworth. She was sitting on her front porch. She was shelling peas. She was all dressed up in her diamonds.

Later that day, I went to her house. My mother said I should invite her to have supper with us.

The porch was empty. The shades were all pulled down. It looked as if no one was home. I rang the bell. After a long time, I rang it again.

The door opened a crack. It was Mrs. Wigglesworth. She poked out her head. She did not seem happy to see me.

"Yes?" she said. "What do you want?"

Her voice sounded funny. Like she was just getting over a sore throat.

I introduced myself.

"Hello," I said. "I'm Audrey Futterman. My mother would like you to come and have supper with us. We live next door."

I was very polite. But Mrs. Wigglesworth said no. She didn't invite me in. She didn't offer me a cookie or anything. When I tried to peek into her house, she closed the door in my face.

Is that the way for a new neighbor to act? I will tell you in one word. No. There was something fishy about Mrs. Wigglesworth. And I was going to find out what it was.

From that day on, I watched her.
Wherever Mrs. Wigglesworth went, I went.
Except when she drove away in her truck. Or
went inside and locked her door.

She drove away in her truck every day. I
wondered where she went. So one day, I
climbed into the back. I hid under a blanket.
Soon, Mrs. Wigglesworth came out of her
house. She got into the truck, and we drove
away.

I peeked out from under the blanket. I wanted to remember where we went. So I drew a map, and wrote down the names of all the streets we were on. I had a notebook and a pencil with me. I am always prepared.

We drove for a long time. The neighborhood began to change. The houses and buildings looked old.

MAIN

At last, we stopped. Mrs. Wigglesworth hopped out of the truck. She went into an old building. I wondered where she was going with all those diamonds. But I didn't follow her. To tell you the truth, I was too scared.

When she came out, a man was with her. I recognized him. It was the Kangaroo. He loaded some boxes onto the truck. I could see him through the blanket. But I didn't move. I lay as still as a dead rat. Except for my heart.

The Kangaroo said, "See ya tomorrow."

Mrs. Wigglesworth answered, "See ya."

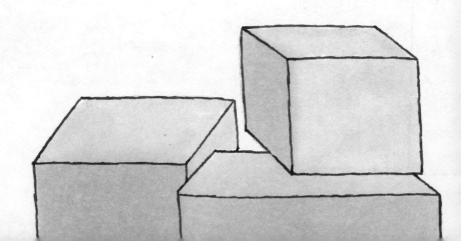

Then she got into the truck. She started the motor, and we drove home.

While she was unloading the boxes, I escaped.

I ran home, and went straight to my room. I had a lot to think about.

The next day, I took a measuring cup and paid a call on Mrs. Wigglesworth. She was as friendly as ever.

"Well?" she said. "What is it now?"

I smiled. A very friendly smile.

"I would like to borrow a cup of sugar, please," I said.

She wanted to say no. But she didn't. She took the cup.

"All right," she grumbled. "But wait here. Don't move. I'll be right back."

She went to get the sugar. She left the door open. Just a crack. But it was enough. When I thought it was safe, I sneaked inside.

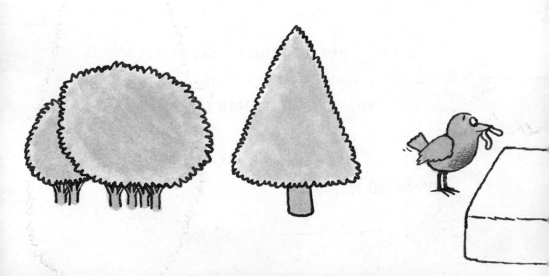

Suddenly, I heard footsteps. I ducked into the nearest room. You could have knocked me over with a feather.

There were about one million television sets in that room. Every single one of them was turned on. Mrs. Wigglesworth was a TV nut!

I decided not to wait. I was almost to the door, when I heard her mumbling.

"Drat that brat!" she said.

I ducked into the bathroom. A razor and a can of shaving cream were on the sink. I wondered who they belonged to.

I looked behind the shower curtain. The house was full of surprises. On the wall was a shelf. On the shelf were a couple of red wigs!

Something weird was going on! I had to get out of there. Fast!

I heard her open the front door. "Where is that nosy brat?" she muttered. I held my breath and didn't move.

At last, she closed the door. She went back to the television room. I pictured her sitting there, watching a million different programs. All at once.

She didn't hear me leave.

I thought about calling the police. But what could I say? I needed more evidence. But evidence of what?

I decided to search the truck.

I waited. My chance came the next morning. Mrs. Wigglesworth went out to mail a letter.

I watched till she was out of sight. Then I cut through the garden. I crawled through the hedge, and crept up her driveway.

There was nothing in the back of the truck.

I looked up in the front. There was a shoe on the floor. It was a man's shoe. I looked under the seat for the other one.

I found it. When I pulled it out, a newspaper came with it.

There was nothing special about the shoe. It was brown. Size 10D. Not too big. Not too small. It was the newspaper that was special.

On page one, there was a story about a gang of jewel thieves. A woman, whose diamonds had been stolen, described one of the thieves:

"He was very tall," she said. "He wore a cap. He had big feet and a fat stomach."

There could be no mistake. It was the Kangaroo!

There was a picture of the leader of the gang. His name was Diamond Dick Macy. He looked familiar. The story said that Diamond Dick had two passions. Diamonds and television.

I remembered the television room in
Mrs. Wigglesworth's house. I remembered
her diamonds. I remembered the red wigs.
Then I remembered the shaving cream in
her bathroom.

I called the police. I told them about the Kangaroo. I told them about my map. Then I told them about Mrs. Wigglesworth.

Everyone was shocked. Mrs. Wigglesworth was not Mrs. Wigglesworth. She was the biggest jewel thief in the country. She was none other than Diamond Dick Macy in disguise. I wondered what she had done with my measuring cup.

It so happens there was a reward. The mayor made a speech. My mother hugged me. My father kissed me. They both said they were proud of me. They also said if I ever did such a dumb thing again, they would lock me in my room for a thousand years.

The other day, I saw an ad on the back
of a matchbook. It said: SO, YOU HAVE
ALWAYS WANTED TO BE A PRIVATE
EYE! There was an address to send away to
for more information.

Guess what I did?
I sent away for more information!

Who knows what might happen?